Mor

the
Spooky Sorceress

Tony Mitton
Illustrated by Arthur Robins

CRAZY CAMELOT

MEET THE KNIGHTS OF THE ROUND TABLE:

King Arthur
with his sword so bright,

Sir Percival,
a wily knight.

Sir Kay,
a chap whose hopes are high,

Sir Lancelot,
makes ladies sigh.

Sir Gawain,
feeling rather green,

Sir Galahad,
so young and keen.

Sir Ack,
who's fond of eating lots,

Sir Mordred,
hatching horrid plots.

Morgana,
Arthur's wicked
sister,

Merlin.
That's me,
your wizard mister!

To courtly Katie Chapman and her courteous uncles, Ben and Dick, from Scribe Tony

To Sir Hayden Thomas Skerry, from Arthur Robins

ORCHARD BOOKS
96 Leonard Street, London EC2A 4XD
Orchard Books Australia
32/45-51 Huntley Street, Alexandria, NSW 2015
First published in Great Britain in 2004
First paperback edition 2004
Text © Tony Mitton 2004
Illustrations © Arthur Robins 2004
The rights of Tony Mitton to be identified as the author
and Arthur Robins as the illustrator of this work
have been asserted by them in accordance with the
Copyright, Designs, and Patents Act, 1988.
A CIP catalogue record for this book is available
from the British Library.
ISBN 1 84121 496 5 (hardback)
ISBN 1 84362 002 2 (paperback)
1 3 5 7 9 10 8 6 4 2 (hardback)
1 3 5 7 9 10 8 6 4 2 (paperback)
Printed in Great Britain

In the days of good King Arthur
when vests were made of chains,
the castle pong was rather strong
'cos they hadn't invented drains.

In fact, at Castle Camelot
there wasn't a single loo.
You just used holes
    in the cold stone walls
for what you had to do!

And if you wanted water
you'd draw it from the well,
unless you practised sorcery,
for then you'd use a spell.

I am the wizard Merlin,
so I know all about it,
and when you've heard my latest tale
I'll bet you will not doubt it.

Just let me tune my crystal ball
to make the picture clear.
I'll need to shake the crackles out -
Aha! The story's here...

It's about King Arthur's sister,
the witch Morgana La Fay,
who cooked up evil magic
to get her wicked way.

"I'll have that goody-goody," she hissed.

I'll fix that little pest.
Why should he rule the kingdom?
He always gets what's best!

She was jealous of her brother,
and keen to grab his power.
So she dreamed up dreams and
    schemed up schemes
in her wicked witch's tower.

My story starts with Arthur
who was hunting with Sir Ack,
when ahead they spied a ghostly deer
a short way up the track.

"Let's chase that deer," King Arthur said.
"It's such a wondrous sight!"
And the two of them rode after it
till - oh! to their delight...

...they found themselves beside a lake
where a luxury boat was moored.
And a lovely lass called out to them,
"Hey, guys! Come right aboard!"

We are the Lakeside Ladies.
Could you fancy a river ride?
There's a picnic here and cans of beer,
so why not step inside?

Sir Ack was always hungry,
so now he licked his lips.
"Ooh look," he said, "there's garlic bread
and, *hey!* tortilla chips!"

The boat looked so inviting
and the Ladies looked so nice
that Ack and Arthur climbed aboard -
they didn't need asking twice.

They lounged on comfy cushions
while the Ladies served them food.
And a minstrel played sweet music
as they nibbled and sipped and chewed.

"Well, doesn't this beat hunting?"
said Arthur to Sir Ack.
"Yes, didn't we get lucky?"
his friend said, leaning back.

And the boat slid oh so gently
over the watery deep
that before too long the minstrel's song
had lulled both knights to sleep.

When Arthur woke up later
he mumbled, "What's that smell?"
And then he sat bolt upright.
"Good Lord! A prison cell!"

I've woken up in a dungeon.
That boat was a cunning trick.
I wonder where Sir Ack has gone?
Crikey! I feel sick...

"I've got to break this horrid spell.
Now how can I escape...?"
Then, by the door King Arthur saw
a spook in a long black cape.

"I've brought you here by magic
to help me in my plight.
Your mega sword Excalibur
could surely win the fight.

"So, if you face this villain,
pretending to be me,
and get to win, and do him in,
well, then we'll both go free.

"But if, by some misfortune,
your opponent wins the fight,
this prison here, for year on year,
will be locked up good and tight."

"There's something dodgy here,"
    said Arthur,
as he thought it through.
"But I'll give the duel a shot," he sighed,
"for what else can I do?"

King Arthur dressed in the dreary gear
of the spooky Dungeon Lord,
then strapped on Great Excalibur,
his trusty magic sword.

And when the Mystery Knight showed up
they both stepped out to scrap.
"Who could this be?" thought Arthur.
"He seems an OK chap."

After some fancy footwork,
King Arthur whacked the bloke.
And, strange to say, well, blimey - *hey!*
Excalibur's blade broke.

And then the other guy whacked back
with a stroke so strong and true
that Arthur's sturdy armour
just let the blade right through.

"Now, just a sec," thought Arthur,
"my scabbard's lost its force.
My magic sword is broken...
The penny's dropped! Of course..."

"This contest is a set up.
The whole darn thing's a trick.
Hold on. Alright? Please pause the fight
to check the weapons. Quick!"

You've got the real Excalibur.
The one I had was a dummy!
I've just been gored with *my* own sword,
and, *ouch!* it hurt my tummy!

The Mystery Knight seemed puzzled.
He gulped and seemed to crack.
He took his great big helmet off
and there stood good Sir Ack!

"But if this sword's Excalibur,"
he murmured, "you're the King!
And yet you fight me in disguise?
This is the weirdest thing!"

"And I could say the same to you,"
said Arthur to his friend.

I think some nasty trick's been played,
or else I'm round the bend.

"This is my wicked sister's work,"
he growled. "I have no doubt.
I'll bet that Dungeon Lord was her.
Let's go and sort this out."

They went back to the dungeon
to see if she was there.
But as they knocked upon the door
it melted into air.

"Another sneaky scam," cried Ack.
"But look! There goes La Fay,
surrounded by her servants -
don't let her get away!"

Arthur and Ack found horses
to follow on her trail.
They rode through bogs and forests,
then reached a misty vale.

"I think they're here," breathed Arthur.
"I feel it in my bones."
But all that they could see there
was a bunch of funny stones.

La Fay had used her sorcery
to turn her gang to rock.
"That's funny," mused King Arthur
and gave her head a knock.

"This boulder's like my sister.
It seems to have her face."
"You're giving me the shivers,"
said Ack, "let's leave this place.

"Besides, I'm getting hungry.
I think my supper's due.
I hope the pot at Camelot
is hubbling up some stew."

The boulders seemed to echo
with Morgana's eerie cackle.
"You're right," replied King Arthur.
"This gang's too weird to tackle."

So back they went to Camelot
and told their chilling tale.
The other knights sat listening
with brimming mugs of ale.

But as the tale was ending
the door went *Rat-Tat-Tat!*
"It's very late," said Arthur.

A servant fetched the visitor,
a girl who gave a smile,
and said, "I come to see the King.
I've journeyed many a mile.

"I bring the King a message
from sorceress Morgana.
She says she's very sorry
and she's been a real banana!

"And just to make it up to him
and give her bro a lift,
she's used her magic well for once
to make a special gift."

She fiddled with the fastenings
of a packet, while she spoke.
Then, with a flourish, out she pulled
a shimmery, twinkling cloak.

"Get this! A cape of wonders,
a garment for a king!
There never was a cloak like this.
It's such a groovy thing!

"So please forgive your sister
and wear her funky cloak.
This is the way she wants to say
that you're an OK bloke."

But Arthur looked suspicious
and said,

Before I do,
I'll just make sure it's safe to wear
by trying it on you.

He swung it round her shoulders
and draped it down her back.
Its sparkle seemed to vanish.
The cape turned shiny black.

And there, before King Arthur,
Morgana stood and scowled.
"I thought this was another trick.
And I was right," he growled.

"Of course," she hissed in fury.
"One day I'll bring you down.
And when I do, then you'll be through,
and I shall wear the crown."

But now the cape was smoking.
It made Morgana twitch.
"Eeeow!" she said, while turning red.
"These hot spells really itch!"

The fatal cape began to glow
and form a shimmering haze.
And then Morgana turned to flames
and vanished in a blaze.

King Arthur kicked the ashes
and pointed to them, "See!
If I'd have put that cloak on
those cinders might be me!"

And I'll bet it's not all over.
If I know her, it's plain
she'll work some spell to make her well,
then pester me again.

"Don't worry, Sire," said good Sir Ack.
"My sister's just as bad.
Whenever she goes on at me
she drives me raving mad.

"But seeing all those cinders
has sparked a good idea.
Let's have a late-night barbecue
with lots of jolly beer."

Ah well, that's it for now, my friends.
That's all I've time to tell.
And, lo! it's Merlin's turn to show
he too can do a spell.

So see me conjure up a hat
all shimmery and hot.
I perch it neatly on my head
and frazzle on the spot!

And now I'm just a little heap
of smouldering ash and ember -
but what's the spell for changing
    back...?
Ooh-er...I can't remember...

CRAZY CAMELOT CAPERS

Written by Tony Mitton
Illustrated by Arthur Robins

Crazy Camelot Capers are available from all good bookshops,
or can be ordered direct from the publisher:
Orchard Books, PO BOX 29, Douglas IM99 1BQ
Credit card orders please telephone 01624 836000
or fax 01624 837033
or e-mail: bookshop@enterprise.net for details.

To order please quote title, author and ISBN
and your full name and address.
Cheques and postal orders should be
made payable to 'Bookpost plc'.
Postage and packing is FREE within the UK
(overseas customers should add £1.00 per book).

Prices and availability are subject to change.